T4-AKW-533

Lauriat's
BOOKS
BOSTON · CHESTNUT HILL
RTHSHORE · SOUTHSHORE

SHIPSHAPE BOY

by
Melvern Barker

CHARLES SCRIBNER'S SONS NEW YORK

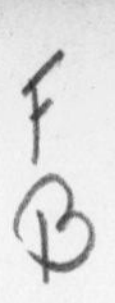

to my own little dog

"Schnapps"

who watched me draw

day after day

A-8.61 [AJ]

Printed in the United States of America
Library of Congress Catalog Card Number 61-13377

While the little red tug boat waited at the dock
for a job to do,

Little Tom and his father Captain Tom were busy making things shipshape. And what is shipshape? To know all about boats of course. To be clean and neat and ready to go when a big boat calls.

Day after day
little Tom practiced things he must know.

He wanted to be shipshape—
but it was so hard to be.

Then one morning while mopping the deck,

Little Tom looked up and saw a puppy.
"It would be fun to be shipshape
if I had a dog," he thought.

So he asked for one. But his father said,
"No, you are too busy to care for a dog.
Maybe some day you can have one."
"How long is some day?" asked little Tom.
Captain Tom laughed.
"When you are shipshape," he said.

Little Tom worked harder and harder.
When he coiled a rope one morning,
he asked his father,
"Am I shipshape now?"

"Not yet,"
said Captain Tom.

And a half hitch was hard to make.
He ran to show what he could do.
"Am I shipshape now?" he asked.

"No," said Captain Tom.
"But you are learning
more each day."

Little Tom began to wonder,
"Will I ever be shipshape?"
when suddenly,
three loud whistles blew.

A big boat was calling
and the little red tug was ready to help.

It was shipshape—
out of the harbor it steamed.

JUDY. B.
CHILMARK

And little Tom steered. He remembered what his father had told him—to pass the red buoys and the black buoys that marked the channel way. It was fun to watch the bobbing boats.

And as he passed the lighthouse,
the children waved.

Soon they were alongside a great white ocean ship. "Throw us a line," shouted the Captain. "Can we throw that high?" asked little Tom. "Yes," said big Captain Tom. "Because our line is coiled properly. We are ship-shape." And zing up-up-up went the line to the very top of the ocean ship.

And the little red tug boat
pulled the big white boat into the dock.

And the ocean Captain came to visit. "Come aboard," said little Tom. "I will show you our tug."

"This is our fo'castle—
where we eat and sleep."

"So clean and neat,"
said the Captain.

"This is our engine room—
see our big motor?"

"And it's ready to go,"
said the Captain.

"And this is the deck, where I work hard
every day. See what I can do—
throw a life preserver and coil it in."

"This is the most shipshape tug
I have ever seen,"
said the ocean boat Captain.
"But something is missing."

"What is missing?"
asked little Tom.

And quicker than you could say it, the Captain ran off. And before you could guess why— he was back with a puppy dog under his arm.

"This little dog got on my boat by mistake," he said. "He is a stowaway—I think he would like to live on a little red tug boat."

"But I can't have a dog," said little Tom.
"Why not?" asked the ocean boat Captain.
"I have to wait 'til some day when I'm shipshape,"
answered little Tom.

Then Captain Tom came into sight
and he began to laugh—a big booming laugh.
"When you can coil a line, tie a knot,
steer a boat, and throw a life preserver,"
he bellowed, "you are ready to take care of a dog.
Because you are a shipshape boy."

"Ahoy," shouted little Tom.
"Some day has come at last."

And down the deck he ran
with his very own puppy dog.
He was the happiest shipshape boy
on the whole waterfront.